LEGACY PUBLICATIONS

# Shackles

By *Marjory Heath Wentworth*

*Illustration by Leslie Darwin Pratt-Thomas*

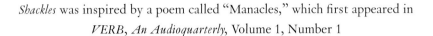

*Shackles* was inspired by a poem called "Manacles," which first appeared in
*VERB, An Audioquarterly,* Volume 1, Number 1

*To Jeff and Taylor - with all my love, gratitude and respect.* — LDP-T
*To my sons Hunter, Oliver and Taylor. Thank you for the inspiration.* — MHW

*In memory of Elmore Brown*

LEGACY PUBLICATIONS, 1301 Carolina Street, Greensboro, NC 27401 / *www.Legacypublications.com*
Printed in Canada by Friesens

*Sullivan's Island* where we live is like a giant playground for me and my brothers. There's a beach where we go swimming and boogie-boarding almost every day.

Across the street from our house there's an old war bunker with a library inside. We like to run around on top of the flat roof, where the sweetgrass grows, and catch worms and lizards. There are caves up on the hill behind the bamboo forest. About a mile down the street is Fort Moultrie, where we run through the tunnels and make believe we're firing cannons on the enemy ships.

My name is Hunter, and I'm old enough to ride my bike to the fort with my friends. We go there almost every day after school. And near the creek behind my house, we built a really cool fort of our own.

*My little brothers,* Oliver and Taylor, are always dressed in costumes. It really drives me crazy. Everyone thinks they're twins, but they're not. My mom says they're Irish twins. I don't know what that means, but I think it means they're *almost* twins.

When Taylor was 2, he never took off his Batman hood and cape. He even slept in them. We still call him "Bat Tay." Last summer, they were both firemen. The hose was on a lot because they were always putting out make-believe fires. "As long as they don't light any real fires, it's fine by me," Dad used to say.

*Today is the day* my brothers are going to dig for buried treasure in the backyard. This summer, they are treasure hunters! My mom is paying me to help watch them, so I have to be real nice. I promised not to tease them. This is going to be hard.

I'm looking for treasure too, but my brothers don't know that. I'm going to use the metal detector that my grandparents sent for my 11th birthday. My grandmother says that our backyard is a treasure trove of metal memorabilia – Civil War coins and slave medallions worth lots of money. Our next-door neighbor Mr. Green says it's true, and since he knows more than anyone else about this place I believe him.

*"Grab the shovels, guys,"* yells Oliver as he rushes down the rickety porch stairs of our old Carolina gatehouse. There used to be a huge mansion in back of our house, but it was washed away in a hurricane. My parents think it's cool that the "gatehouse" built for slaves and servants is the one still standing.

"We're coming!" Taylor tumbles out the side door, his arms wrapped around a big red beach bucket and shovel. He is squinting in the sunlight. I get the garden shovel from the shed and hand it to Oliver. It is bigger than he is, but he smiles.

"Thanks, Hunt," he says. "If you help us, we'll share some of the gold."

"Sure, Oli, whatever." I grin to myself. I can smell the salt coming in off the ocean. Our island is so narrow that no matter where you are, you can always hear the waves and smell the sea.

*Seagulls sit* on the beam across the swing set. "Look at those gulls, you guys, they are the lookouts!"

"Excellent, we need lookouts." Taylor salutes the gulls. He is only 5, but he always uses big words like *excellent*. All the adults say he's really smart. He's funny, too. Who else would salute a bunch of birds?

*But Oliver is* in charge of this project! He is 6 years old, after all, which is one year older than Taylor, he reminds us.

"Here, Hunter, here." Oliver points to a place near the swing set where the little banana tree used to be. "See, the big *X* on the map, that's where the pirates buried the treasure when they were shipwrecked off of Sullivan's Island."

The first grade has just gone on the annual end-of-school field trip to The Pirate Museum in Charleston. Oliver bought a map there that tells where treasure was buried on barrier islands.

"Wow," exclaims Taylor, unrolling the crinkled parchment. "See, this is our street, and this is our backyard!" He is so excited that he jumps up and down.

*After a few minutes*, William, Jeffrey, and Jacob show up – shovels in hand. William and Jeffrey are wearing black pirate hats with a skull and crossbones on the front.

"Cool hats, you guys," I say, even though I think they're kind of silly.

"We got them at Patriot's Point on Memorial Day," Jeffrey says proudly.

My little brothers have agreed to share their treasure with anyone who helps them dig. Two weeks ago, in a neighbor's yard, they found a wooden door with the knob still attached, pieces of a broken plate, and the skeleton of an animal that they're certain is a werewolf. I told them it's Jacob's old dog Jenny, but they don't believe me for a minute.

*"Aren't you guys* dying in this heat?" I ask. "I swear it's over a hundred degrees."

"Don't bother us, Hunter, we're working." Oliver looks up from the hole, sweat streaming down his red face.

"I'm going inside to get some drinks from Mom, be right back." I run in the house, and Mom is standing at the kitchen window watching the boys digging a huge hole in the backyard. I wonder if she's angry.

"They are determined, aren't they," she sighs. "Here, bring these juice boxes out to them before they faint. Make sure that hole doesn't get any bigger, one of them might fall in."

Wow, she isn't angry at all!

"Hey, guys, here's something to drink," I yell. They ignore me as if they can't even hear. Oliver and Jacob are standing in the hole pulling hard on something I can't see. Whatever it is, it's covered in dirt. Oliver hands something to Taylor, and he almost drops it.

"What is it? What is it?" All the boys are crowded around Taylor now. "Chains or something?"

He hands me an armful of mud and metal. It is all as heavy as bricks, and I almost drop it.

*Jacob has grabbed* the hose, and he starts rinsing off the rust and mud. "Aren't these slave handcuffs?" he asks.

"Well, kind of," I whisper, then I yell, "MOM." She waves through the window, and it looks like she's on the phone. All the boys are crowded around me. They look disappointed. This isn't the treasure they were looking for.

*"All right, then*, go get Mr. Green, he'll know what this is," I say hopefully.

Oliver runs next door and returns with Mr. Green. It looks as if Oli is pulling him by the hand, but he has a big soft smile on his face so it's okay. Mr. Green was born on Sullivan's Island, and he knows more about this place than anyone in the world. He tells us stories about how everyone lived off the land and had little farms with animals. There wasn't a bridge to the mainland. Half the families were African-American, and the other half were white. Everyone took care of each other, and all the kids played together and ran around the island just like us. But when they started school, they were separated by color, which he didn't understand then and still doesn't understand.

"Look, Mr. Green, look what we found on our treasure hunt." Jacob holds the "handcuffs" up for Mr. Green to see.

"Shackles," he says softly, shaking his head. His big grin disappears, and he looks very old to me all of a sudden.

"Shackles? What the heck are shackles?" Taylor looks up and pulls on Mr. Green's pants.

*"You know, slave shackles,"* I try to explain. Taylor shakes his head, bewildered.

"You boys know that slaves used to be here, before the Civil War," Mr. Green says. "They were kept on the island under quarantine in the pesthouse before they were sold downtown at the market."

Taylor is shaking his head again. "What are slaves?"

"Well, slaves were Africans who were kidnapped by white men and brought here on ships to work against their will. This island is the first place many of the ships stopped."

"Africans, what? My cousins are Africans." Taylor is fuming. "So what are these shackle things? I don't get it." He looks like he's going to cry.

"That was long ago. You know what prisoners are, Taylor." Mr. Green is touching the shackles while he talks softly. His hands are shaking. "The slaves were prisoners, and they were locked in these shackles so they couldn't escape."

All the little boys are standing in a circle around us. Jeffrey reaches up and touches them. "Creepy," he says, "really creepy."

There are tears on Mr. Green's cheeks. "Creepy, that's right, Jeffrey."

*Taylor has started* crying, too. Mr. Green holds Taylor's hand, and they don't say anything for a few minutes. Then Mr. Green stoops down and faces Taylor and says, "When I was your age I didn't understand that much about cruelty either. It's better that way. Once you recognize it, you find it everywhere you go. You have to learn to find its opposite – kindness. You can find that everywhere you look, too."

*"Here, you keep these shackles,"* I say to Mr. Green.
Oliver lifts them from Jacob's hands and places them in Mr. Green's hands.
He gathers them up and holds them close to his chest.
   "What are you going to do with them?" Oli asks the question we are
all wondering about.

*"I don't know.* Maybe I'll give them to a museum. Maybe not. Burying them deep down in the earth isn't such a bad idea either." Mr. Green says this so quietly we can barely hear him. He walks back toward his house alone.

*Mr. Green comes over* for dinner that night.
Even after he and my parents have explained as much as they can
about slavery and the Civil War and lots of things they want us to
understand about history, Taylor still cannot be convinced that slavery
could have happened here in his own backyard. He wants to call his
Nigerian cousins Tarieye, Disaye, and Ebi and warn them about the bad guys
from Charleston who have something to do with pirates, and could be,
for all he knows, on a boat right now on their way to Africa to kidnap them
and bring them to Sullivan's Island. The island where slaves were held by
the thousands before they were sold or buried, here in the backyard
of our house, on the island where we live.